Dear Dragon Goes to the Market

by Margaret Hillert
Illustrated by David Schimmell

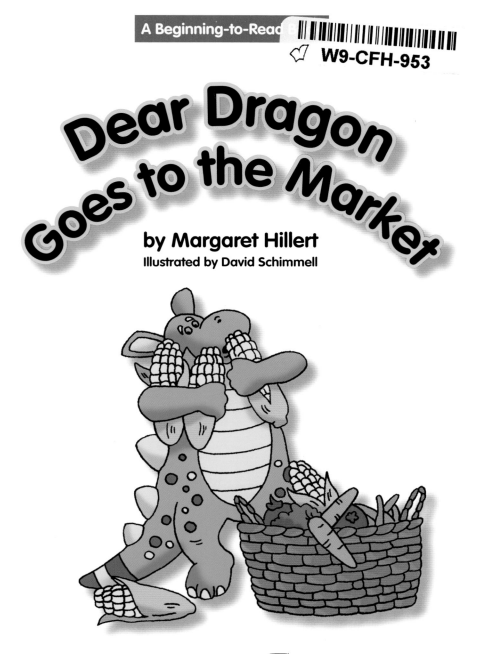

NORWOOD HOUSE PRESS

The **Dear Dragon** series is comprised of carefully written books that extend the collection of classic readers you may remember from your own childhood. Each book features text focused on common sight words. Through the use of controlled text, these books provide young children with abundant practice recognizing the words that appear most frequently in written text. Rapid recognition of high-frequency words is one of the keys for developing automaticity which, in turn, promotes accuracy and rate necessary for fluent reading. The many additional details in the pictures enhance the story and offer opportunities for students to expand oral language and develop comprehension.

Shannon Cannon

Shannon K. Cannon, Ph.D.
Literacy Consultant

Norwood House Press • P.O. Box 316598 • Chicago, Illinois 60631
For more information about Norwood House Press please visit our website at *www.norwoodhousepress.com* or call 866-565-2900.
Text copyright ©2011 by Margaret Hillert. Illustrations and cover design copyright ©2011 by Norwood House Press, Inc. All rights reserved. No part of this book may be reproduced or utilized in any form or by any means without written permission from the publisher.

Paperback ISBN: 978-1-60357-097-8

The Library of Congress has cataloged the original hardcover edition with the following call number: 2009031725

Manufactured in the United States of America in North Mankato, Minnesota.
295R—062016.

I have to get something
for us to eat.
Do you want to go with me?

There is a good spot.
You will see.
Come on. Come on.

Oh, oh—
Look at all this!

You can do this.
It will be a big help.

Yes, Mother.
We can help you.
We like to help.
This will be fun.

These are green BEANS.
Yes, we want some.
BEANS are good for us.

And look here.
Oh, boy! APPLES!
Can we get some APPLES?

Yes.
We will get some APPLES.

The TOMATOES are red.
They are so good to eat.
We will get TOMATOES, too.

TOMATOES

17

Now what can we get, Mother?

HONEY

JELLY

JAM

SQUASH

CHERRIES

CUCUMBERS

POTATOES

CARROTS

PEPPERS

TURNIPS

CELERY

Do you like CARROTS?
We can get CARROTS.

CARROTS

Oh, yes.
I like CARROTS.
Big, orange CARROTS.

There is something yellow.
Yellow CORN.
Can we get some CORN?

I guess so.
It can go in here.

I want something pretty, too.
Look for something pretty.

There, Mother. There.
See the pretty FLOWERS.
You can get FLOWERS.

Yes, we will get FLOWERS.
Now we can go.

Here you are with me.
And here I am with you.
What a good day, dear dragon.

WORD LIST

Dear Dragon Goes to the Market **uses the 61 pre-primer and 7 new vocabulary words listed below.** This list can be used to practice reading the words that appear in the text. You may wish to write the words on index cards and use them to help your child build automatic word recognition. Regular practice with these words will enhance your child's fluency in reading connected text.

a	get	oh	want
all	go	on	we
am	good		what
and	green	pretty	where
are	guess		will
at		red	with
	have		
be	help	see	yellow
big	here	so	yes
boy		some	you
	I	something	
can	in	spot	
come	is		**New**
	it	the	**Vocabulary**
day	like	there	**Words**
dear	look(s)	these	
do		they	apples
dragon	me	this	beans
	Mother	to	carrots
eat		too	corn
	now		flowers
for		us	orange
fun			tomatoes

ABOUT THE AUTHOR Margaret Hillert has written over 80 books for children who are just learning to read. Her books have been translated into many different languages and over a million children throughout the world have read her books. She first started writing poetry as a child and has continued to write for children and adults throughout her life. A first grade teacher for 34 years, Margaret is now retired from teaching and lives in Michigan where she likes to write, take walks in the morning, and care for her three cats.

Photograph by Glenna Washburn

ABOUT THE ADVISOR Shannon K. Cannon is a teacher educator, staff developer, and curriculum writer. She earned her doctorate in Language, Literacy, and Culture from the University of California Davis, where she serves on their clinical faculty supervising pre-service teachers, teaching elementary methods courses in reading/language arts and technology, and teaching Master's courses in inquiry. She began her career teaching second grade. She then spent over 15 years in educational publishing where her work included developing and writing curricular programs as well as providing professional development support to classroom teachers.

ABOUT THE ILLUSTRATOR David Schimmell served as a professional firefighter for 23 years before hanging up his boots and helmet to devote himself to working as an illustrator of children's books. David has happily created illustrations for the New Dear Dragon books as well as the artwork for educational and retail book projects. Born and raised in Evansville, Indiana, he lives there today with his wife and family.